# CLEVER C

## Learns to Obey

Bob Hartman
Illustrated by Steve Brown

DAVID C COOK®

*transforming lives together*

CLEVER CUB LEARNS TO OBEY
Published by David C Cook
4050 Lee Vance Drive
Colorado Springs, CO 80918 U.S.A.

Integrity Music Limited, a Division of David C Cook
Brighton, East Sussex BN1 2RE, England

Library of Congress Control Number 2023939764
ISBN 978-0-8307-8593-3
eISBN 978-0-8307-8617-6

© 2024 Bob Hartman
Illustrations by Steve Brown. Copyright © 2024 David C Cook

The Team: Laura Derico, Stephanie Bennett, Judy Gillispie, James Hershberger, Karen Sherry
Cover Design: James Hershberger
Cover Art: Steve Brown

Printed in China
First Edition 2024

1 2 3 4 5 6 7 8 9 10

060223

Clever Cub stamped his foot. "I don't **WANT** to do it!"

Papa Bear frowned. "But you really hurt Skippy Squirrel when you PUSHED him out of that tree."

"It was an accident!" grunted Clever Cub.

"Hmm. That's not what Fred said. Right, Fred?"
Papa Bear stared hard at Fred the bunny and Clever Cub.
"Now, Clever Cub, do what I say. **OBEY**. Go tell Skippy
you are sorry."

"But it is so-o-o **HARD** to do," Clever Cub whined. "Everyone will make fun of me!"

"It is not always **EASY** to obey. But God wants us to learn how to do it. It's hard for me too, you know."

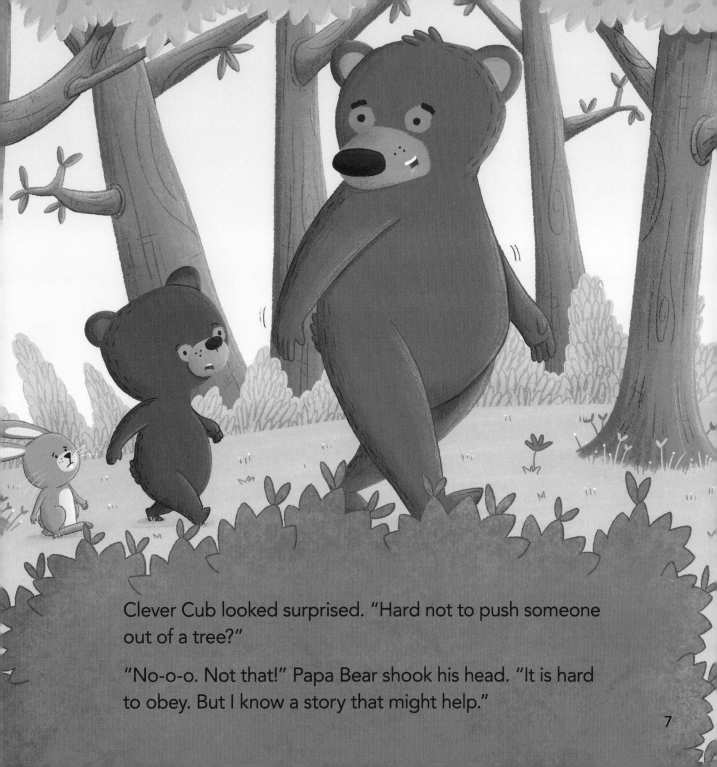

Clever Cub looked surprised. "Hard not to push someone out of a tree?"

"No-o-o. Not that!" Papa Bear shook his head. "It is hard to obey. But I know a story that might help."

7

"A Bible story?" Clever Cub asked. "I **LOVE** Bible stories!"

"That's right!" Papa Bear said. "This story is about a prophet called Elisha (ee-LIE-shuh) and a man called Naaman (NAY-mun). Naaman was a powerful army commander for a country called Syria. But he had a **TERRIBLE** skin problem."

"That sounds awful! But at least he did not have to obey anyone. He was the **BOSS**!" Clever Cub shouted out.

Papa Bear smiled. "Well, even army commanders must learn to obey. But we'll get to that part."

"First, you need to know that Naaman had a servant girl. She was taken from her home in Israel when Naaman and his soldiers invaded the land."

"That sounds even **AWFULLER!** Naaman was not very nice!" Clever Cub stamped his foot again.

"Maybe not. But the servant girl was **VERY** nice to Naaman and his family," Papa Bear said.

"She **OBEYED** God's commands about showing love to others, especially to people from other lands. She told Naaman's wife about a prophet of God who could heal Naaman's skin."

"Elisha?" Clever Cub guessed.

"Exactly! You *are* a clever cub!"

Papa Bear went on. "Naaman wanted to be healed right away. He took soldiers and horses and chariots all loaded with **TREASURE** and set off to ask the king of Israel for Elisha's help. The king did not want to help Naaman. But Elisha said, 'Send the man to me!' And the king did.

"When Naaman got to Elisha's house, however, Elisha did not even come out! He sent a **MESSENGER** instead."

"What did the messenger say?" Clever Cub asked.

"He said, 'Dip yourself **SEVEN** times in the Jordan River, and you will be healed.'"

Clever Cub scratched his nose. He was thinking about how much he liked to splash in the river. "That sounds **EASY**! Did Naaman do it?"

"Well, it was not so **EASY** for Naaman. He wasn't used to obeying, remember? He was powerful. He didn't want to look weak. Obeying some man he didn't know in a strange land would have been **HARD** for him. And probably embarrassing too," Papa Bear said.

"In fact, Naaman was **ANGRY**. 'This prophet should have stood before me and called on God and waved his hand over me,' he said. 'We have beautiful rivers back home in Syria. Why should I wash in some dirty river in Israel?!'

"Naaman turned away from Elisha's messenger and walked off in a **RAGE**."

"Oh no!" Clever Cub looked worried.

"Oh yes," Papa Bear said. "But Naaman's servant spoke up: 'Master, if the prophet had challenged you to do a **HARD** thing, you would have done it. Why not do this **EASY** thing? Obey the man of God, wash in the river, and be healed!'

"So-o-o, Naaman obeyed! And when he came up the seventh time—"

"His skin problem was gone!" Clever Cub shouted.

"All **GONE**!" Papa Bear nodded. "Naaman was so happy, he told Elisha he would obey the God of Israel from then on. Naaman learned that obeying God is good to do, even when it's hard."

"Hard—like telling Skippy I'm sorry?" Clever Cub said.

"Exactly!" Then Papa Bear encouraged his cub: "Why not go and tell him now?"

"I will! And then I am going to dip in the river—way more than **SEVEN** times!"

# For Clever Readers

Clever Cub is a curious little bear who **LOVES** to cuddle up with the Bible and learn about God! Clever Cub didn't want to obey his papa or God. It seemed so hard! But when he heard the story about Elisha and Naaman (from 2 Kings 5:1–19), he found out that obeying God is sometimes easier than we think. And it's always good to do.

When is obeying hard for you? When is it easy?

If you ask God, He will help you obey. Then you can be as happy as a bear cub in a river! What do you need to ask God for help with today?